The Wild · Little · Horse

BY **Rita Gray** · ILLUSTRATED BY **Ashley Wolff**

Dutton Children's Books · New York

To Logan and Nell,
who love horses so well
R.G.

For Sara Reynolds,
whose care and creativity make every book a joy
A.W.

———————

DUTTON CHILDREN'S BOOKS
A division of Penguin Young Readers Group
Published by the Penguin Group

Penguin Group (USA) Inc., 375 Hudson Street, New York, New York 10014, U.S.A.
Penguin Group (Canada), 10 Alcorn Avenue, Toronto, Ontario, Canada M4V 3B2
(a division of Pearson Penguin Canada Inc.)
Penguin Books Ltd, 80 Strand, London WC2R 0RL, England
Penguin Ireland, 25 St Stephen's Green, Dublin 2, Ireland
(a division of Penguin Books Ltd)
Penguin Group (Australia), 250 Camberwell Road, Camberwell, Victoria 3124, Australia
(a division of Pearson Australia Group Pty Ltd)
Penguin Books India Pvt Ltd, 11 Community Centre, Panchsheel Park, New Delhi-110 017, India
Penguin Group (NZ), Cnr Airborne and Rosedale Roads, Albany, Auckland 1310, New Zealand
(a division of Pearson New Zealand Ltd)
Penguin Books (South Africa) (Pty) Ltd, 24 Sturdee Avenue, Rosebank, Johannesburg 2196,
South Africa
Penguin Books Ltd, Registered Offices: 80 Strand, London WC2R 0RL, England

LIBRARY OF CONGRESS CATALOGING-IN-PUBLICATION DATA
Gray, Rita.
The wild little horse/by Rita Gray; illustrated by Ashley Wolff.—1st ed.
p. cm.
Summary: Little Horse cannot resist the call of the wind, which encourages him to run like a
wild colt and cavort by the sea.
ISBN 978-0-525-47455-5
[1. Horses—Fiction. 2. Play—Fiction. 3. Wind—Fiction. 4. Seashore—Fiction. 5. Stories in rhyme.]
I. Wolff, Ashley, ill. II. Title.
PZ8.3.G7438Wi 2005
[E]—dc22 2004024515

Published in the United States by Dutton Children's Books,
a division of Penguin Young Readers Group
345 Hudson Street, New York, New York 10014
www.penguin.com/youngreaders
Designed by Jason Henry
Manufactured in China • First Edition
3 5 7 9 10 8 6 4

A little horse with eyes so wide
watches the world that waits outside.

The pile of wood, the pile of hay,
the field of grain where little mice play.
SKITTER SKIT SKITTER SKIT

His mama and papa twitch their tails
and sip cool water from an old tin pail.
SWISH SWISH SWISH

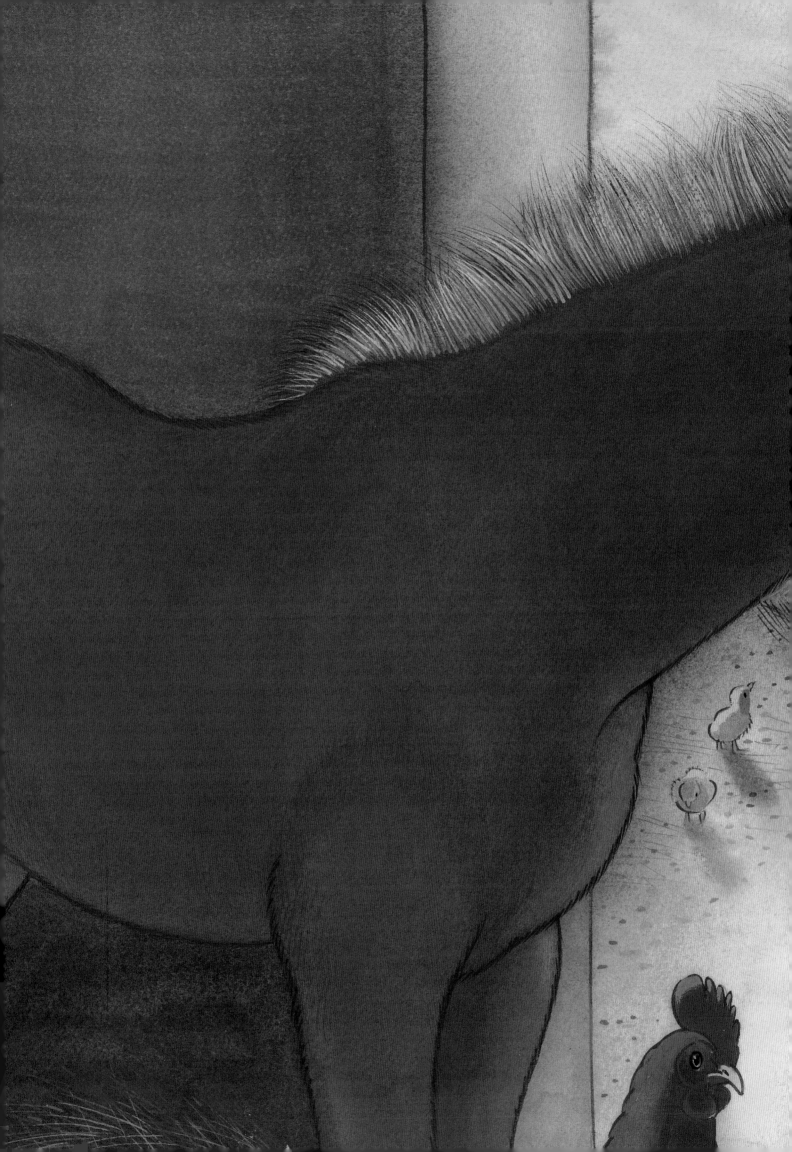

Then up from the field, past the wood, past the hay,
a whistling wind comes winding his way.
And Little Horse has the wind in his ears;
whistling wind is all he hears.
WHOOSH   WHOOSH
He hears it blow past;
it's calling him now to run so fast!

And even though he's not full grown,
Little Horse wants to roam.
His mama and papa give a gentle neigh.
Go, Little Horse, the wind knows the way.

So off he trots, not very far,
looking to see where the others are.
But the lambs are sleeping in the sun,
and cow is really too big to run.
But ducks on the grass
sometimes move fast,
so Little Horse goes racing there
and sends them flapping in the air.
QUAAAAACK!

And now he's off, racing past,
running, running, running fast!
He runs with the wind held in his mane,
a wild horse, no longer tame.
GALLIPITY-LIP GALLIPITY-LOP
This wild horse might never stop!

But now his nostrils start to flare;
he smells a wetness in the air.
That special smell he loves so well,
of sand and salt and waves that swell.
He runs with the wind, so wild and free,
all the way to the rolling sea.

SPLASH! RUMBLE-RUSSHHH
SPLASH! TUMBLE-GUSSHH
As *he watches the waves rise and fall,*
he feels so small,
just a little horse after all.

But the sea is calling with shimmering sun,
Come, Little Horse, come in and run!
So he sets off into the froth…
step, step, step,
one more step and he's…
WET! WHINNY! WHEEEEEE!
Little Horse in the giant sea!

Romping, stomping, pawing the ground,
Little Horse is horsing around!
Then up pops a seal, shiny and dark,
calling up close with his deep seal bark.
ARK ARK ARK ARK
They run and swim, side by side,
then the seal goes out with a tug of the tide.
But now Little Horse has birds to chase,
a crowd of birds to send someplace!

He finds a pool filled with the tide
and sees a horse with eyes so wide—
a horse who's looking very grown,
out in the world, out on his own.

Then through the waves and salty spray,
Little Horse hears a familiar neigh.
And he sees them both standing there,
his big Papa Horse, his own Mama Mare.
With one last leap in the frothy foam,
they toss their heads and race for home.

And they run, they run, they run like the wind,
past the waves and rocking shore,
back to the world as slow as before.
The ducks, the cows, the lambs so still,
all the way to their own quiet hill.

He nuzzles them close, right in between,
then settles onto his soft bed of green.
And Little Horse has the wind in his ears;
whispering wind is all he hears.

Good night, wild horse, the sky has dimmed.
Tomorrow you'll wake and run like the wind.